W9-BKE-035

Questions and Answers: Countries

Scotland

A Question and Answer Book

by Janeen R. Adil

Consultant:
Candace Groskreutz
Assistant Director, Center for British Studies
University of California, Berkeley

Capstone
press

Mankato, Minnesota

Fact Finders is published by Capstone Press
151 Good Counsel Drive, P.O. Box 669, Mankato, Minnesota 56002.
www.capstonepress.com

Library of Congress Cataloging-in-Publication Data
Adil, Janeen R.
    Scotland : a question and answer book / by Janeen R. Adil.
    p. cm.—(Questions and answers: countries)
    Includes bibliographical references and index.
    ISBN–13: 978–0–7368–6773–3 (hardcover)
    ISBN–10: 0–7368–6773–2 (hardcover)
    1. Scotland—-Juvenile literature. I. Title. II. Series.
DA757.5.A35 2007
941.1—dc22
                                                      2006028502

Summary: Describes the geography, history, economy, and culture of Scotland in a
    question-and-answer format.

Editorial Credits
Silver Editions, editorial, design, photo research and production; Kia Adams, set designer;
    Maps.com, cartographer

Photo Credits
Alamy/David Lyons, 21; Food Features, 25; Iain Masterton, 13; Jennie Hart, 27
Corbis/Dave Bartruff, cover (foreground); George Steinmetz, 15; Ric Ergenbright, 1;
    Sandro Vannini, 4; Tim Graham, cover (background)
Getty Images Inc./Peter Sandground, 23; Stone/Roy Giles, 18; Taxi/Andrew Shennan, 11
The Image Works/SSPL/National Railway Museum, 17; Topham, 9; Topham/Miller, 19
Library of Congress, 8
Mary Evans Picture Library, 7
One Mile Up, Inc., 29 (flag)
Paul Baker, 29 (coins)

Table of Contents

Features

Where is Scotland?

Scotland is located in northern Europe. It shares the island of Great Britain with England and Wales. Scotland is a bit smaller than the U.S. state of South Carolina. It has a cool and damp climate.

Scotland also includes 787 smaller islands. Most are part of island groups called the Shetland, Hebrides, and Orkney Islands.

Lakes in Scotland are called lochs. *Here, an old castle looks out across Loch Ness.*

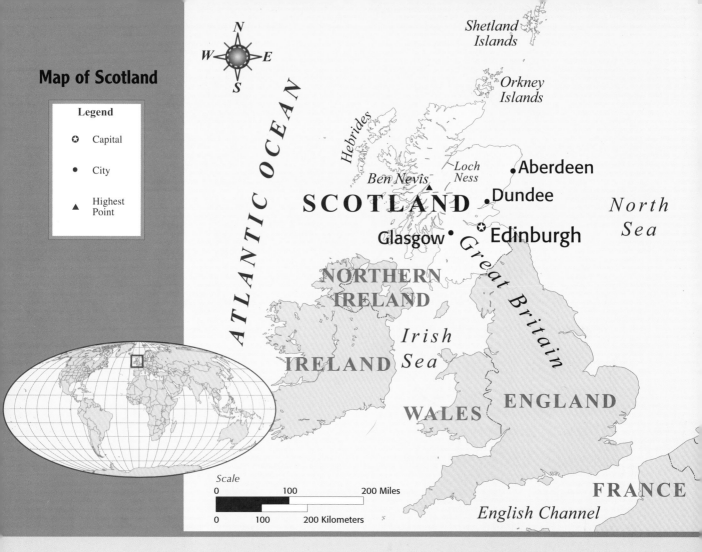

Map of Scotland

Legend

✪ Capital

• City

▲ Highest Point

N
W   E
S

ATLANTIC OCEAN

Shetland Islands

Orkney Islands

Hebrides

Loch Ness

Ben Nevis ▲

SCOTLAND

•Aberdeen

•Dundee

Glasgow•

✪ Edinburgh

North Sea

Great Britain

NORTHERN IRELAND

Irish Sea

IRELAND

WALES

ENGLAND

FRANCE

English Channel

Scale

0   100   200 Miles

0   100   200 Kilometers

Scotland has three main regions. In the north are the mountains of the Highlands. A wide valley crosses the center of the country. Most Scottish people live there. Hills to the south divide Scotland and England.

When did Scotland become a country?

Scotland's first king was crowned in 843. This event brought two tribes together into one kingdom. Centuries later, England tried to take land from Scotland. In 1314, the Scottish fought and defeated the English army.

Scotland was free but not at peace. The country battled England many times for another 300 years. Fights between Scottish **clans**, or family groups, also spread from the Highlands across the country.

Fact!

Scotland's earliest kings sat on a stone block when they were crowned. This famous rock is called the Stone of Scone, or the Stone of Destiny.

Scottish fighters had crude weapons and little armor. Even so, they fought bravely against the English army.

In 1603, King James VI of Scotland became King of England, too. In 1707, the Act of Union joined the two nations and Wales as Great Britain. Today, Great Britain is joined with Northern Ireland as the United Kingdom (UK).

What type of government does Scotland have?

Scotland, along with the rest of the United Kingdom, is a **constitutional monarchy**. A king or queen is the head of state. An elected government makes laws for the UK. These representatives form a group called a **parliament**. The prime minister is the leader of the elected government.

Fact!

Before joining the United Kingdom, Scotland was a monarchy with its own kings and queens. Mary, Queen of Scots, was one of the most famous. Her son James became King of England in 1603.

Scotland's government meets in Holyrood, a building with modern architecture.

In 1997, Parliament passed the Scotland Act. Some power to govern was **devolved**, or passed back, from the UK to Scotland. Scotland's leaders formed the **Executive** in 1999. The Executive governs most parts of Scottish life. The First Minister leads the Executive.

What kind of housing does Scotland have?

In Scotland's cities, many people live in apartments called flats. Some live in large housing blocks called row houses and council houses. In towns, homes for single families are often made of brick or stone. Houses can cost a lot in Scotland. Many old homes have historic value.

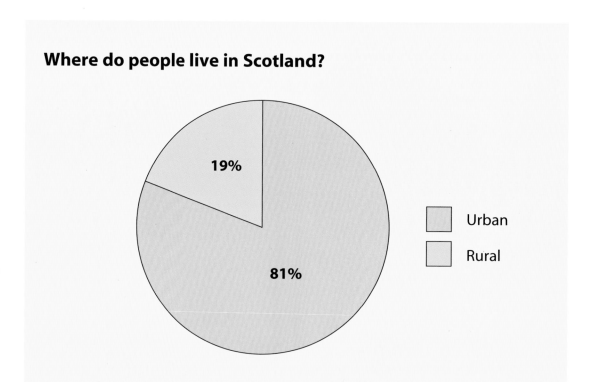

Where do people live in Scotland?

19%

81%

Urban

Rural

Small shops take up the ground floor in these apartment buildings in Edinburgh, Scotland's capital.

People in the Highlands and islands often live on crofts, or small farms. A croft house has thick stone walls. Tightly packed hay or straw on the roof protects families from the harsh weather.

What are Scotland's forms of transportation?

Scotland's railways and roads crisscross the country. As in many parts of Europe, cars are often small. Groups of people sometimes share rides in minivans called people movers.

Many Scots rely on trains for travel. Scotland has one subway, the Glasgow Underground. Small orange trains run on a circular route under the city. Its nickname is the "clockwork orange."

Fact!

Thousands of people in Aberdeen rely on helicopters to get to work each day. Their jobs take place on oil rigs in the North Sea. All these flights make Aberdeen the world's busiest helicopter port.

Inner Circle

eet P	Cowcaddens	Kinning Park	Partick ⇄ 🚌
treet P	St Georges Cross	Cessnock	Kelvinhall
⇄ 🚌	Kelvinbridge P	Ibrox	Hillhead
Street ⇄ 🚌		Govan 🚌	

Inner Circle ↙   **Outer Circle** ↘

Shields Road

Scotland's only subway system may be small, but Glasgow residents rely on its efficiency.

Because they live on an island, Scots also travel by air and sea. Major airports are located in big cities like Glasgow and Edinburgh. Ferries carry people and cars to and from Scotland's many islands. Boats also take people to other countries in Europe.

What are Scotland's major industries?

Scotland's factories provide many of the country's jobs. Some factories make aircraft parts. Others make chemicals. Fabrics, clothing, and electronic equipment are all made in Scotland, too. Factories sell and ship these products all over the world.

In the 1960s, oil and natural gas were discovered under the cold, rough North Sea. Underwater pipelines carry the oil and gas to shipping centers. Some of the world's biggest oil companies have offices in Aberdeen.

What does Scotland import and export?	
Imports	**Exports**
food	oil and natural gas
computers (hardware)	computer software
cars	chemicals

A worker repairs the drill of an oil rig platform in the North Sea.

Scotland also has a growing service and **tourism** industry. Each year, millions of people visit Scotland to see the ancient castles and beautiful scenery. They stay at hotels of all sizes and enjoy meals in many local restaurants.

What is school like in Scotland?

All children in Scotland receive a free public education. Students study math, reading, writing, and many other subjects. The school year is divided into an autumn term and a spring term. Then students enjoy a summer vacation.

Scottish students usually wear uniforms to school. These clothes show the school's colors and feature a special school badge.

Fact!

The University of St. Andrews in Fife was founded in 1413. England's Prince William graduated from the school in 2005.

Scottish students wear their school jerseys on a field trip to learn more about history and geography.

Younger students go to primary school. Students attend secondary school from ages 12 to 16. They must then pass exams before continuing for one or two more years. Some students take exams called Highers to attend a college or university.

What are Scotland's favorite sports and games?

Soccer has been Scotland's national sport for hundreds of years. Most towns and cities have **professional** teams that play one another. Scotland's team also plays in the World Cup.

Every year, Scots gather at various sites for the Highland Games. The Games began hundreds of years ago as traditional clan gatherings. People compete in events such as running, jumping, hammer throwing, and weight tossing.

Fact!

The caber toss is the highlight of the Highland Games' sports. The caber is a heavy tree trunk about 16 to 20 feet (5 to 6 meters) long. The player tosses it end-over-end.

The golf course in St. Andrews calls itself the "Home of Golf."

Many people claim that Scotland invented golf in the 1400s. Even Scottish kings and queens enjoyed playing the game. The first British Open was held in Prestwick in the early 1860s. Today, most towns and cities in Scotland have a golf course.

What are the traditional art forms in Scotland?

The bagpipes are Scotland's national instrument. Bagpipers once led the Scots into battle. Their loud, strong sound can be heard for miles. Today, bagpipers and drummers often perform together at popular events.

Highland dancing is a Scottish tradition. This lively dance requires great skill and strength. There are many special steps to learn. At the Highland Games, children and adults compete in dancing contests.

Fact!

Robert Louis Stevenson and J. K. Rowling are famous Scottish writers. Stevenson's classic book Treasure Island *continues to delight young readers, much like Rowling's books in the* Harry Potter *series.*

Bagpipe players and drummers often perform in groups called military tattoos to honor the history of the music.

Scottish craftspeople use sheep's wool to weave plaid cloth called **tartan**. It is used to make kilts. The skirt-like kilt is part of a Scottish man's traditional clothing. Each clan has its own plaid pattern and colors.

What holidays do people in Scotland celebrate?

Scotland celebrates most major Christian holidays. That wasn't always so. For hundreds of years, the Church of Scotland said that people should work on Christmas. Now most people have the day off.

Hogmanay is an ancient Scottish version of New Year's Eve. Today, it includes bonfires, parties, and street festivals. At midnight, people gather and sing "Auld Lang Syne" to remember the past.

What other holidays do people in Scotland celebrate?

Easter
Halloween
Boxing Day

Many people dress up in historical costumes to celebrate the passing of time during Hogmanay.

Burns Night takes place on January 25. It honors Scotland's famous poet Robert Burns. Guests eat traditional Scottish foods at dinner. Afterward, they listen to bagpipe music and read the poetry of Burns aloud.

What are the traditional foods of Scotland?

Scots enjoy hearty foods. Meats are eaten at most meals. Angus beef, lamb, and game birds are popular. Salmon, trout, haddock, and herring are favorite fish.

Basic vegetables and grains round out the menu. Potatoes, called tatties, carrots, and cabbage are traditional foods. Turnips, called neeps, are also popular. Oats are used to bake bannocks, or oatcakes. They are also used for porridge, a thick breakfast oatmeal.

Fact!

In many schools, Scottish children can buy snacks at a tuck (food) shop. They can choose from fruit, cereal bars, crisps (potato chips), plain popcorn, fruit juice, and water.

Haggis is often served with chips, which Americans commonly call French fries.

Haggis is a traditional Scottish dish from ancient times. Haggis looks like sausage and tastes like meatloaf. Chopped sheep organs are mixed with oatmeal and onions. This is then stuffed into a bag made from a sheep's stomach. The bag is then boiled for hours.

What is family life like in Scotland?

Family life in Scotland has changed over the centuries. Clans play a smaller role in making choices for family members. Marriage is not as common as it once was. Scottish families today are usually small with only one or two children. Many children have a stepfather or stepmother.

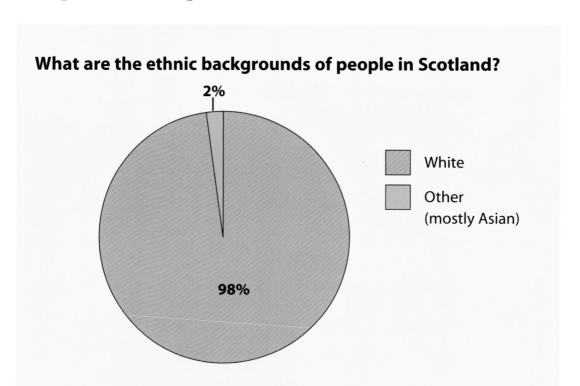

What are the ethnic backgrounds of people in Scotland?

2%

98%

White

Other (mostly Asian)

Today, people in Scotland spend more time in small family groups and less time together as a clan.

In the past, many young Scots moved to other countries to find jobs. Today, more young people are staying in Scotland to live and work. They share a strong feeling of pride in their country's past and future.

Scotland Fast Facts

Official name:

Scotland (part of the United Kingdom)

Land area:

30,418 square miles (78,782 square kilometers)

Average annual precipitation (Edinburgh):

26.6 inches (67.6 centimeters)

Average January temperature (Edinburgh):

38.3 degrees Fahrenheit (3.5 degrees Celsius)

Average July temperature (Edinburgh):

58.1 degrees Fahrenheit (14.5 degrees Celsius)

Population:

5,078,400 people

Capital city:

Edinburgh

Languages:

English (official), Scots Gaelic, Scots

Natural resources:

coal, hydroelectric (water) power, oil and gas

Religions (Scotland):

Church of Scotland	42%
Roman Catholic	16%
Other Christian	7%
Muslim	<1%
Jewish	<1%
Other/None	33%

Money and Flag

Money:

Scotland's money is the Scottish Pound Sterling. In early 2006, 1 U.S. dollar equaled 0.58 pounds sterling. One Canadian dollar equaled 0.50 pounds.

Flag:

Scotland's flag is the cross of St. Andrew, the country's patron saint. The flag has an X-shaped white cross on a blue background. It is one of the oldest flags in the world. The Royal Flag of Scotland is a second national flag. This flag has a red lion on a yellow background.

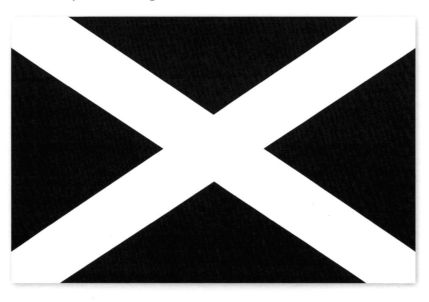

29

Learn to Speak Scots Gaelic

English is spoken throughout Scotland. Scots Gaelic is the historic language for most of the country. Today, you can hear it mostly on the islands and in the Highlands.

English	Scots Gaelic	Pronunciation
Welcome!	Fàilte!	(FAHL-chuh)
good morning	madainn mhath	(MAH-tin VAH)
How are you?	Ciamar a tha thu?	(KIM-mar uh HAH oo)
I'm fine	Tha mi gu math.	(hah mee guh MAH)
good-bye	mar sin leat.	(MAR SHIN LEHT)
thank you.	tapadh leat	(TAH-pah LEHT)

Glossary

clan (klan)—a large group of families and related people

constitutional (kon-sti-TOO-shuh-nuhl)—having to do with an important set of rules or laws, as for a nation

devolve (dee-VAWLV)—to pass on from one person or group to another

Executive (ig-ZEH-kyuh-tiv)—the top level of government in Scotland

monarchy (MON-ahr-kee)—a system of government in which the ruler is a king or queen

parliament (PAHR-luh-muhnt)—a group of people elected to make laws

professional (pruh-FEH-shuh-nuhl)—a person who makes money by doing an activity that other people might do without pay

tartan (TART-uhn)—wool cloth with a plaid pattern

tourism (TOOR-i-zuhm)—the business of taking care of visitors to a country or place

Internet Sites

FactHound offers a safe, fun way to find Internet sites related to this book. All of the sites on FactHound have been researched by our staff.

Here's how:
1. Visit *www.facthound.com*
2. Choose your grade level.
3. Type in this book ID **0736867732** for age-appropriate sites. You may also browse subjects by clicking on letters, or by clicking on pictures and words.
4. Click on the **Fetch It** button.

FactHound will fetch the best sites for you!

Read More

Britton, Tamara L. *Scotland.* The Countries. Edina, Minn.: Abdo, 2003.

Cane, Graeme, and Lise Hull. *Welcome to Scotland.* Welcome to My Country. Milwaukee: Gareth Stevens, 2002.

O'Sullivan, MaryCate. *Scotland.* Faces and Places. Chanhassen, Minn.: Child's World, 2002.

Richardson, Hazel. *Life of the Ancient Celts.* Peoples of the Ancient World. New York: Crabtree, 2005.

Index